11-08

FRIENDS
OF ACPL

W9-DIZ-135

THIS BOOK BELONGS TO:

. . . .

nach Pourquoi why? P
porqué TXε Waarum
Proč hvorfor? Pam
waarum
why?
为什么 hvorfor 为什么? nach
Proč hvorfor Pourquoi? Proč perché?
Pourquoi nach nach Proč 为什么?
Pourquoi Proč TXε Porqué Perché
waarum cur why Proč Whwhy
niçin Pourqu
niçin why dlaczego hvorfor niçin
niçin warum
Proč why niçin? ljls? Pourqoowhy
ljls 为什么 why niçin yiari hvorfor? perqué niçin Proč
why Pourquoi Proč TXεnach nach cur Wh
yiari niçin Proč Pourque? Pourqoui Pourquoi niçin
Niçin ljlz? Pam ljlz nach why P
roč Pourquoi hvorfor niçin why P
why 为什么 dlaczego Perqué cur why
ljlz Proč pour qoboi pourquoi why 为什
Proč nach hvorfor ljls
why Pourquoi proč Pam why yiari Perqué пoy
vorfor niçin warum why hvorfor Pam
perqué nach yiari Waarum why Pam
why Почему TXε Perqué? why Pow
why 为什么 why why
为什么 dlaczego Pam Pourquoi niçin niç

nicin hvorfor why why why nicin
uczego warum Pam
nach why? Perqué yiari? nicin Pam Porqu
hvorfor Proč Pourgoi Pourquoi? why why? Pro
pam nicin hvorfor hvorfor Warum Perche
yiari warum nicin Pourquoi
Proč waarom Proč why
why Why Why? why porque pourquoi why Joyem
dlaczego? yiari Why pourquoi why Why
why Proč pourquoi nach why Proč
nach waarom why?
rquoi? yiari nach yiari pam why why
cur pourquoi dlaczego nicin Proč why
yiari dlaczego nicin Proč cur
yiari waarom Proč? Perqué
aczego Proč yiari Proč Pour quoi? Perche Pro
yiari warum nicin nach Why
nicin Proč dlaczego
nicin? Pourquoi dlaczego Pam
why why why Proč
perche nach why

For Laura. Why? It just is - L.C.

For Abigail and Penguin - T.R.

First published in Great Britain in 1998 by Andersen Press Ltd., 20 Vauxhall Bridge Road, London SW1V 2SA.
This paperback edition first published in 2008 by Andersen Press Ltd.
Published in Australia by Random House Australia Pty., Level 3, 100 Pacific Highway, North Sydney, NSW 2060.
Text copyright © Lindsay Camp, 1998. Illustration copyright © Tony Ross, 1998
The rights of Lindsay Camp and Tony Ross to be identified as the author and illustrator of this work have been
asserted by them in accordance with the Copyright, Designs and Patents Act, 1988.
All rights reserved. Colour separated in Switzerland by Photolitho AG, Zürich.
Printed and bound in Singapore by Tien Wah Press.

10   9   8   7   6   5   4   3   2   1

British Library Cataloguing in Publication Data available.

ISBN 978 1 84270 607 7

This book has been printed on acid-free paper

Why?

written by **LINDSAY CAMP**

illustrated by **TONY ROSS**

ANDERSEN PRESS

There was one thing Lily did that drove her dad mad.

Actually, it wasn't a thing she *did*.

It was a thing she said.

She said it all the time.

She said it first thing in the morning.

It's time you were dressed.

Why?

She said it at breakfast time.

Your egg just needs another minute.

Why?

9 4209 05670 8289

She said it when they went shopping.

Mustn't forget to buy some more bin bags.

Why?

She said it when her dad read her a story.

And of course, she said it at bedtime.

Usually, Lily's dad

did his best to explain.

Because it rained all
last night.

Why?

Because there
were lots of big
black clouds full of
tiny drops of water.

Why?

Because . . . well, there
just were, Lily.

There just
were!

But sometimes, when he was a bit tired or too busy,

he'd just get cross.

Then, one Friday, something rather unusual happened.

Lily was playing in the sandpit in the park.

Suddenly, Lily's dad stopped and looked upwards. So did Lily.
And so did everybody else in the park.

Lily was too astonished to say anything. After all, she'd never seen a gigantic Thargon spaceship before.

The Thargon spaceship came lower, and then it landed in the park, right next to the sandpit.

Everybody stood and stared. The doors of the spaceship slid open

and out squelched several Thargons.

They didn't look very friendly.

The most important Thargon oozed forward.

Everyone started to tremble.

Everyone except Lily, that is.

Why?

WHY?
Because that is our
mission, of course.

Why?

Because destroying
puny planets brings
glory to the mighty
Thargon Empire.

Why?

Because . . . well,
because our Great Leader,
the Imperial Tharg, says so.

Why?

Because . . . he just does,
Small Female Earthling,
he just does. Hmmm . . .

The chief Thargon turned to his friends. He looked thoughtful.

Lily and her dad and all the other people watched as they talked together in Thargish for quite a long time.

Then the chief Thargon slithered forward again, and spoke to Lily.

Lily was just about to say something

but her dad put his hand over her mouth,

BYE!
Have a nice day. Sorry
to have troubled you.

just in time.

That night at bedtime, when he'd finished reading her a story,

Lily's dad gave her an extra big hug.

And then he promised he'd never get cross with her again,
no matter how often she asked him why.

I was very proud
of you in the park
today.

Why?

why — warum — pourquoi — porque — proč — waarom — nach — hvorfor — perché — dlaczego — niçin — cur — pam — yiari — perqué — 为什么 — למה

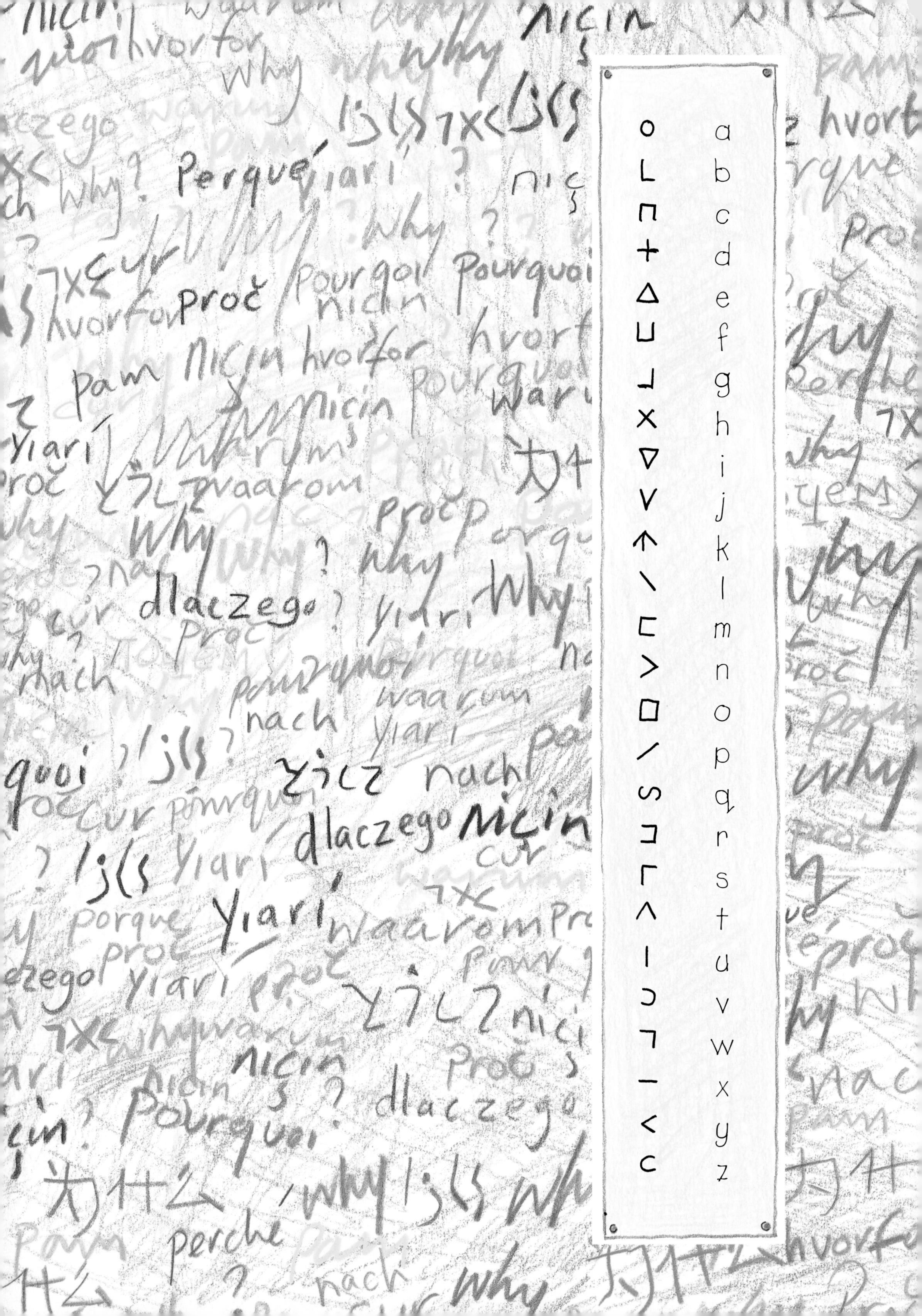
a
b
c
d
e
f
g
h
i
j
k
l
m
n
o
p
q
r
s
t
u
v
w
x
y
z

Also by
LINDSAY CAMP and TONY ROSS:

'As near to perfection in the
sleepytime genre as one could ask.'
T.E.S.

'Will appeal to three-to-seven-year-olds.'
DAILY TELEGRAPH